Red is a dragon
Red is a drum
Red are the firecrackers—
here they come!

In this lively concept book a little girl discovers a rainbow of colors in the world around her: Red is a dragon in the Chinese New Year parade, yellow are the taxis she sees on her street, green are jade bracelets and the crunchy kale growing in her garden. Many of the featured objects are Asian in origin, but all are universal in appeal. With rich, boisterous illustrations, a fun-to-read rhyming text and an informative glossary, this colorful book will brighten every child's day!

"...a welcome addition to preschool story hours for children of all backgrounds."
—*Booklist*

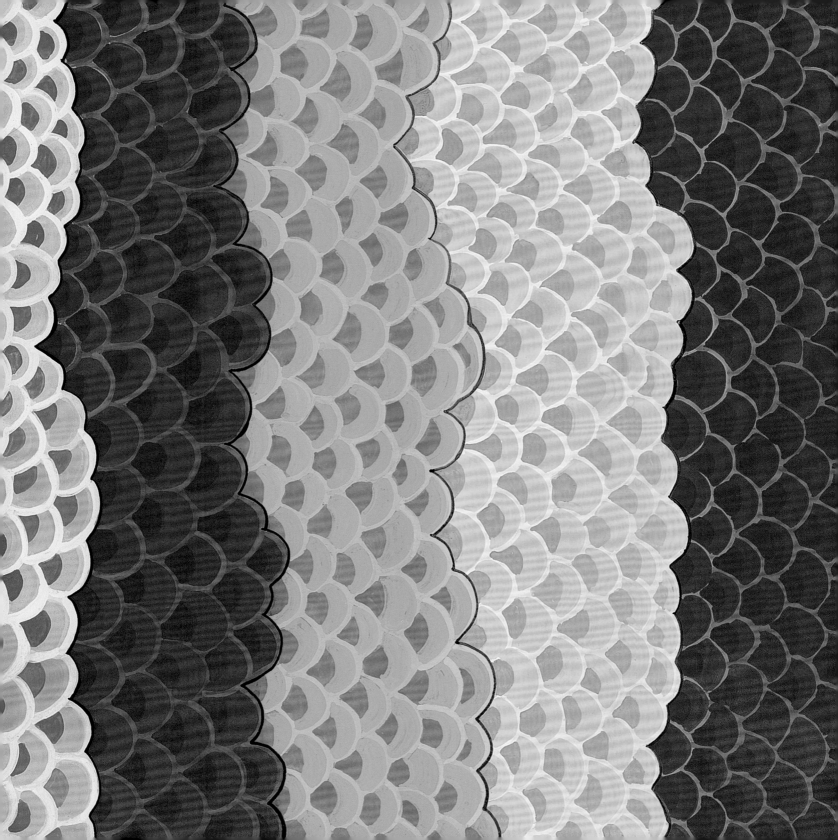

For Foong Sze, Foong Yann, Sheng Zhou and all children
who delight in the colors around them. —R. T.

To Linda S. Wingerter, who, when I asked her to pick a color,
always chose green. —G. L.

First paperback edition published in 2008 by Chronicle Books LLC.

Text © 2001 by Roseanne Thong.
Illustrations © 2001 by Grace Lin.

Book design by Sara Gillingham.
Typeset in Albertus.
The illustrations in this book were rendered in gouache.
Manufactured in China
ISBN 978-0-8118-6481-7

The Library of Congress has catalogued the hardcover edition as follows:
Thong, Roseanne.
Red is a dragon / by Roseanne Thong ; illustrated by Grace Lin.
p. cm.
Summary: A Chinese American girl provides rhyming descriptions of the great variety of colors she sees around her,
from the red of a dragon, firecrackers, and lychees to the brown of ginger, soy sauce, and her teddy bear.
ISBN 0-8118-3177-9
[1. Color—Fiction. 2. Chinese Americans—Fiction. 3. Stories in rhyme.]
I. Lin, Grace, ill. II. Title.
PZ8.3.T328 Re 2001
[E]—dc21
2001000093

20 19 18 17 16 15

Chronicle Books LLC
680 Second Street, San Francisco, California 94107
www.chroniclekids.com

Red Is a

Dragon

A Book of Colors

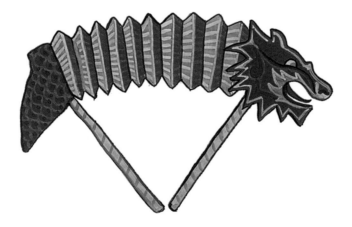

written by Roseanne Thong ❀ illustrated by Grace Lin

chronicle books · san francisco

Red is a dragon
  Red is a drum
Red are the firecrackers—
  here they come!

Red are melons
cool and sweet
Red are lychees
a summer treat

Orange are the crabs
 that dance in the sand
And so is the seashell
 I hold in my hand

Yellow are incense sticks
 and flowers
Yellow are flames
 that burn for hours

Yellow are raincoats
    and bright rubber boots
Yellow is a taxi
    that honks and toots

Green are the toads
beneath my pail
Bottle gourds
and crunchy kale

Green is a bracelet
made of jade
Green is the purse
my auntie made

Blue is a pool
 for making a wish
Dragonflies and
 shimmering fish

Blue are the sneakers
on my shelf
Blue is the ribbon
I won myself

Purple are clouds
  at the end of the day
Purple is a kite
  that sails away

Pink is a peony
Pink is a rose
Pink is the sunlight
on my nose

Pink are an opera
singer's eyes
And a silk fan
that hides her surprise

Brown is my grandpa's
    hat I wear
Brown is my favorite
    teddy bear

White are noodles
and chopsticks, too
White are dumplings
for me and you!

The world is a rainbow
for us to explore
What colors are waiting
outside your door?

SOME OF THE WORDS FOUND IN THIS BOOK

Bottle gourd: A pear-shaped vegetable eaten in soups, stir-fried or boiled. It is often pictured in Chinese design and art.

Chopsticks: Two thin sticks used to pick up food. They are usually made of wood, plastic or bamboo.

Dragon: Chinese dragons help people rather than harm them. A New Year dragon dance brings good luck and scares away evil spirits.

Dumplings: Small pockets of dough filled with meat or vegetables, shaped like half moons.

Firecrackers: Chinese firecrackers are tiny red cylinders that hang in long strings. Their loud cracking noise is thought to chase away bad luck.

Incense sticks: Sandalwood sticks that give off a sweet-smelling smoke when burned. They are used for prayer or worship.

Jade: A hard, usually green- or white-colored gemstone used to make jewelry and art objects. It is thought to offer protection to those who keep it.

Lychee: A small, oval fruit from Southern China that grows on trees and ripens in early summer. It has bumpy red skin and a sweet white translucent center.

Peony: Known as the "queen of flowers," the peony is a popular Chinese flower. It represents springtime and wealth.

Silk fans: Fans have been used in China for more than three thousand years. After the invention of silk, artists and scholars began to decorate silk fans with poetry and pictures.

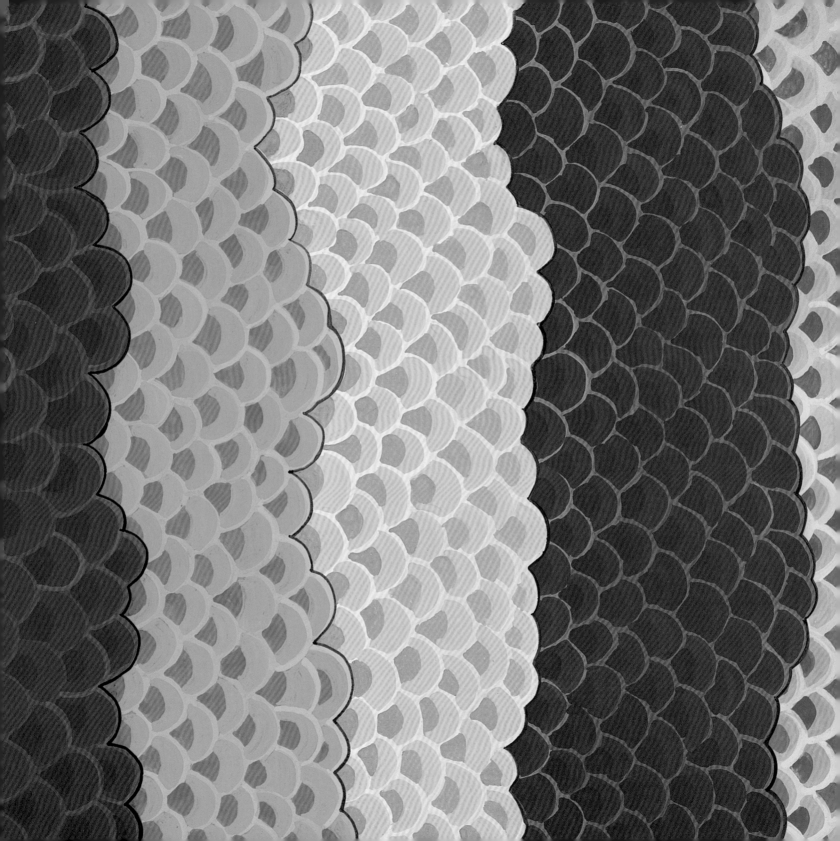

ALSO BY ROSEANNE THONG AND GRACE LIN:

Round Is a Mooncake: A Book of Shapes

"An enchanting primer for children of all backgrounds."
—*Publishers Weekly*

". . . provides a gentle lesson in shapes . . . as well as culture."
—*Booklist*

"A charming and instructive math concept book."
—*Kirkus Reviews*

One Is a Drummer: A Book of Numbers

". . . enormously engaging."
—*School Library Journal*

"An appealing counting book."
—*Booklist*

Roseanne Thong dreamed of colors as a child, which made this book
a pleasure to write. Ms. Thong was born in Southern California,
but now lives in Hong Kong with her husband and daughter.
She writes and teaches English.

Grace Lin graduated from the Rhode Island School of Design. She loves all
bright colors; she even paints in a bright yellow room. Visit Ms. Lin's
Web site at www.gracelin.com.